The No Snow North Pole

Elena Schietinger

Archway Publishing books may be ordered through booksellers or by contacting:

Archway Publishing
1663 Liberty Drive
Bloomington, IN 47403
www.archwaypublishing.com
844-669-3957

Interior Image Credit: Michael Perez

ISBN: 978-1-6657-2853-9 (sc)
ISBN: 978-1-6657-2854-6 (hc)
ISBN: 978-1-6657-2852-2 (e)

Print information available on the last page.

Archway Publishing rev. date: 09/12/2022

This book is dedicated to Cole, for inspiring me always, but especially on a snowy Christmas Eve as we ran out for that one last present.

Way up north,
where it's usually cold,
a strange thing happened
so the story is told.

The snow stopped falling,
it became very warm,
not even a flake,
certainly never a storm.

Santa was worried.
This wasn't much fun.
The North Pole loved snow,
not a big, bright, hot sun!

The elves were unhappy.
They said with a frown,
"The snow is all melting.
No snow's falling down!"

And then those poor reindeer!
The sun made them weak.
How could they fly
and perform at their peak?

Santa sent out a message,
Mother Nature came near,
but all that she said
was so sad to hear.

"The whole world is warming,"
she said with a sigh.
"The North Pole is melting.
I think I might cry."

"But Christmas is coming,"
dear Santa did say.
"I need some cold weather
to fly on my sleigh."

"The reindeer are tired.
The sun makes them sleep.
The elves are unhappy.
They even might weep."

Mother called to the wind,
and the wind called the rain,
and a plan to save Christmas
soon was what came.

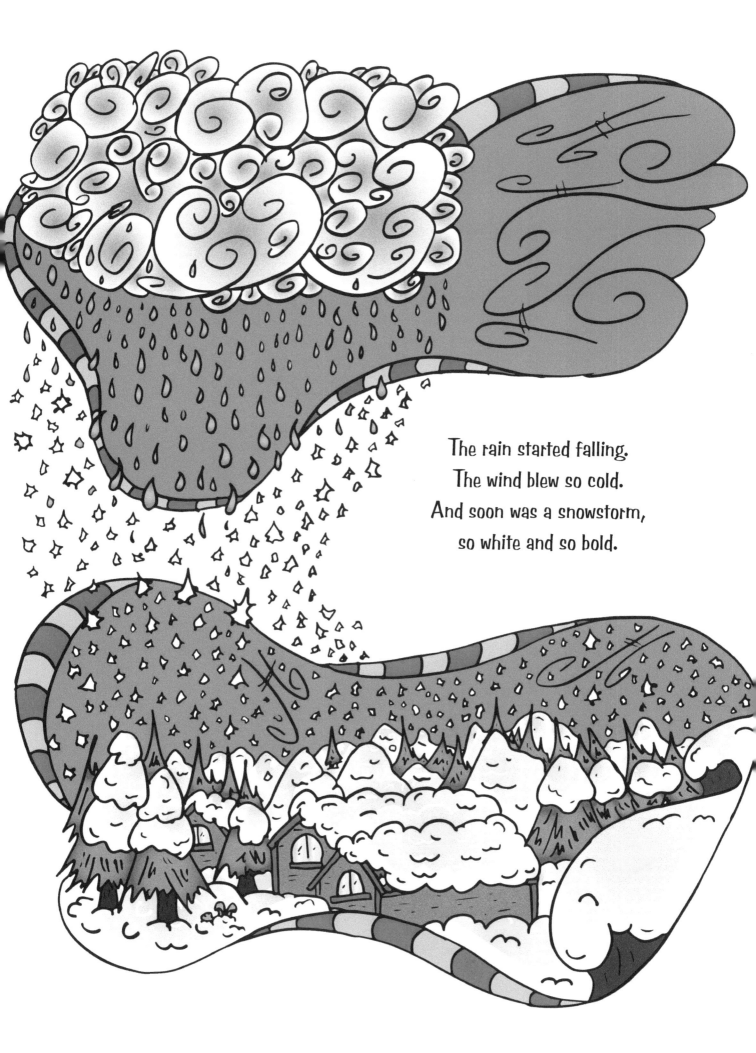

The rain started falling.
The wind blew so cold.
And soon was a snowstorm,
so white and so bold.

Santa was happy
as the snowflakes did fall.
The elves and the reindeer,
they danced one and all.

And then as dear Santa
was loading his sleigh,
Mother Nature called out,
"Please come over my way."

"To keep this place frozen
and have plenty of snow,
the Earth must be happy,
that much you must know."

"The children can help
with this plan if they try.
Then never again
will we see your elves cry."

She took Santa's hand
in her hand and did say,
"Here's dust that is magic
that you'll take on your sleigh."

"Sprinkle the children
as you fly through the night,
then they all will know
what they have to do right."

"Do it each year
so the children will know
how to keep a good balance
between hot sun and snow."

"They'll tell of the time
that the snow didn't fall
because the Earth needed love
from its people, one and all."

The End.

Here are some ways you can show the Earth love:

Don't litter.

Plant trees, fruits, vegetables, and flowers.

Recycle.

Use paper bags.

Don't use plastic straws and bottles.

Support a community garden.

Clean up your community.

Conserve water.

Make a compost pile.

Walk or ride your bike instead of driving.

Carpool.

Pass on to others your gently used toys, books, clothes, and sports equipment.